MY LiFe
as a
Screaming
Skydiver

BOOKS BY BILL MYERS

The Incredible Worlds of Wally McDoogle (18 books)
—*My Life As a Smashed Burrito with Extra Hot Sauce*
—*My Life As Alien Monster Bait*
—*My Life As a Broken Bungee Cord*
—*My Life As Crocodile Junk Food*
—*My Life As Dinosaur Dental Floss*
—*My Life As a Torpedo Test Target*
—*My Life As a Human Hockey Puck*
—*My Life As an Afterthought Astronaut*
—*My Life As Reindeer Road Kill*
—*My Life As a Toasted Time Traveler*
—*My Life As Polluted Pond Scum*
—*My Life As a Bigfoot Breath Mint*
—*My Life As a Blundering Ballerina*
—*My Life As a Screaming Skydiver*
—*My Life As a Human Hairball*
—*My Life As a Walrus Whoopee Cushion*
—*My Life As a Mixed-Up Millennium Bug*
—*My Life As a Beat-Up Basketball Backboard*

Other Children's Series
McGee and Me! (12 books)
Bloodhounds, Inc. (8 books)

Teen Series
Forbidden Doors (10 Books)

Teen Nonfiction
Hot Topics, Tough Questions
Faith Encounter

Picture Book
Baseball for Breakfast

Adult Fiction
Blood of Heaven
Threshold
Fire of Heaven
Eli

Adult Nonfiction
Christ B.C.
The Dark Side of Supernatural

www.Billmyers.com

the incredible worlds of **Wally McDoogle**

MY LiFe as a Screaming Skydiver

BILL MYERS

Thomas Nelson, Inc.
Nashville

Published in Nashville, Tennessee, by Tommy Nelson®, a
division of Thomas Nelson, Inc. Visit us on the web at
www.tommynelson.com

Scripture quotations identified as (NIV) are from the HOLY
BIBLE, NEW INTERNATIONAL VERSION®. Copyright ©
1973, 1978, 1984 International Bible Society.

Library of Congress Cataloging-in-Publication Data

Myers, Bill, 1953–
    My life as a screaming skydiver / Bill Myers.
        p.   cm. — (The incredible worlds of Wally McDoogle ; #14)
    Summary: When Wally becomes involved in international
espionage, rocket-powered toilet paper, and exploding dental
floss, he ends up having to become a skydiver to save his life
and the entire free world.
    ISBN 0-8499-4023-0
[1. Spies—Fiction. 2. Skydiving—Fiction. 3. Christian life—
Fiction. 4. Humorous stories.] I. Title. II. Series: Myers, Bill,
1953–   . Incredible worlds of Wally McDoogle ; #14.
PZ7.M98234 Myi   1998
[Fic]—dc21   98-11458
                                                             CIP
                                                              AC

Printed in the United States of America

06 RRD 15

To Cathy Glass—
for her love and faithful service to
children over these many years.

"Therefore confess your sins to
each other and pray for each other
so that you may be healed. . . ."

—James 5:16 (NIV)

Contents

Chapter 1

Just for Starters . . .

Don't blame me! It wasn't my fault!

Blame my best friend, Opera, the human eating machine. After all, it was his birthday.

Or blame Wall Street, my other best friend (even though she *is* a girl). After all, it was her idea to throw a party at Destructo Lasers. It was her idea for us to play laser tag.

I was just an innocent victim. It wasn't my fault I didn't know how to put on the laser vest.

"No, Wally, it goes over your shirt, not your pants."

And it wasn't my fault I got stuck.

"No, Wally, those holes are for your arms, not your legs!"

After the local paramedics swung by and cut me out of the vest with their Jaws of Life, I tried on another one.

"No, Wally, now you've got it on backward."

(Fortunately the paramedics were still around.)

After the third one, I finally got it right. At last things were getting back to normal. (But, as we all know, normal for me isn't exactly normal for anyone else.)

At first, it was great fun running around the maze of futuristic walls, firing our lasers at each other and scoring points. Well, Opera and Wall Street were running around firing lasers and scoring points. I was too busy getting hit to score anything. It seemed every time I fired my laser, someone was hitting me.

> *Phring Phring Phring*
> *BLAM! BLAM! BLAM!*
> *Phring Phring Phring*
> *BLAM! BLAM! BLAM!*

It was getting pretty frustrating, until Wall Street stopped by and offered a suggestion. "You're holding your laser backward," she shouted over the noise.

"What?" I yelled.

"You've got it turned around! You're shooting yourself!"

I glanced down and saw her point. "Thanks!" I shouted.

"Don't mention it!" she yelled and then stepped back to fire a few good rounds into me.

Phring Phring Phring
BLAM! BLAM! BLAM!

(Hey, we're good friends, but not that good.)

Before I could fire back, she'd dashed around the corner and disappeared.

I tore after her and probably would have gotten her, too—if it wasn't for the six-foot, three-inch, blond man who raced around the corner from the other direction. Even that wouldn't have been so bad, if I hadn't leaped out of his way. Actually, the leaping was pretty good. It was the smashing into the wall that was the problem.

"Oaff!"
K-THUDD

The *"Oaff!"* was my muscle-challenged body hitting the hard wood wall. The *K-THUDD* was my newly broken body hitting the even harder concrete floor.

The blond guy hadn't done much better. By trying not to trample me to death, he also stumbled and fell—just as two other men, a tall guy and a short guy, came barreling around the corner and started firing at him.

As I lay there, flat on my back, counting how many bones I'd broken, I thought how unfair it was that they let grownups play with kids. I mean, I was living proof (well, now semi-living proof) that if you weren't careful, someone could really get hurt (or at least killed). But what I thought was *really* unfair was the way they let the grownups play with real guns.

Play with real guns?!?

K-BLEWY! K-BLEWY! K-BLEWY!

I couldn't believe my eyes or ears. They were shooting real guns at the blond guy! The good news was they seemed to miss every shot. The bad news was they turned the wall behind him into a pile of splinters.

I thought of warning them that the owner could be a little sensitive to this type of behavior and maybe even throw them out. But when I saw the damage their guns did, I figured it might be a good idea not to rile them.

K-BLEWY! K-BLEWY! K-BLEWY!

Now the blond guy was firing back.

Talk about cool! It was just like the movies. Well, except for the part of nearly getting killed. My heart was pounding like a jackhammer on top of a pogo stick in the middle of an earthquake. I flattened myself against the wall and quickly began making deals with God to let me live. I'd barely gotten to the part of promising to empty the trash without being asked when the bad guys ducked around the corner to reload.

The blond guy took advantage of the moment and rolled out of sight into the shadows—just as the two ran back in with their guns blazing.

After turning another wall into kindling, the tall guy shouted at me in a thick accent, "Vhere iz hee?"

I knew it was time to speak up. It was time to do what I did best. It was time to deny everything. "I didn't do it!" I cried. "I was just minding my own business, and he just sort of tripped and—"

The short man interrupted and shouted to his partner, "Hee muust hav gone to zee ozer zide!"

They took off and raced right past me (without so much as a "thank you"—or would it be a "zank you"?) as they continued their pursuit. It was then I heard the blond guy give a quiet groan. I turned around and spotted him crouched in the corner only ten feet away.

"Mister . . . ," I whispered, "Mister, are you all right?"

More groans. I started toward him. "Mister . . ."

When I arrived, he was gasping and trying to get up. "Must . . . stop . . ." But his leg collapsed, and he tumbled back to the floor.

"You're hit!" I cried. "They shot you!"

He looked at me and grimaced. "You!" he gasped in a thick English accent. "You're responsible."

"It's not my fault!" I cried. "I didn't do it!" (I told you I was good at this.)

He shook his head and continued. "Now . . . you must help."

"What?"

Again he tried to stand. "Now you . . . must protect . . ." And again he fell.

"Take it easy," I yelled. "We've gotta get you to a hospital!"

He shook his head violently.

"But you gotta see a doctor!"

Again he shook his head. "Must protect . . ."

"Must protect what?" I cried. "What are you trying to protect?"

"Giggle . . . Gun."

"Giggle *what??*"

"Giggle . . . Gun." It was getting a lot harder for him to breathe, but he forced himself to continue. "World peace . . . at stake . . . must stop them from finding . . ."

"Stop who?" I shouted. "Stop who from finding what? The *Giggle Gun?*"

He nodded, painfully.

"You're not serious."

But I could tell he was very serious . . . *deadly* serious.

"Where . . . where is it?" I asked.

"Cave . . . ," he gasped. "Africa . . ."

"Listen," I explained. "I'd love to save the world, but it's getting close to dinnertime and—"

He reached out a trembling hand and pointed to something on the floor just a few feet away. It was a pack of chewing gum that looked like it had been placed there on purpose.

"Take it," he groaned. "You must take it."

"Uh, no thanks," I said staring down at it. "My mom only lets me chew sugarless."

"You must . . . help. Take it. It's your responsibility. Just add water." And suddenly he collapsed. Just like that. Without even saying good-bye.

"Mister . . ." I knelt down to him. "Mister, wake up!"

But he wasn't in the mood for waking up. Come to think of it, he wasn't in the mood for breathing either.

"Mister, please!" I shouted. "Don't die! I don't want to get any Giggle Gun!"

But he was no longer listening.

Unfortunately, his buddies with the guns were. They had raced around the corner and had heard the last part of my plea. "He'z wiz zee kid!" they shouted.

I thought of sticking around to chat, but since they didn't exactly look in a chatty mood, I grabbed the gum, leaped to my feet and

K-BONK!

ran into the wall. I spun around and

K-BONK!

ran into the other wall.

I had to get out of there. Seconds counted. There was only so much time before the bad guys would stop laughing at my antics long enough to take aim and fill my body with more lead than a number two pencil.

Fortunately, I'd run out of walls. Now I had a clear shot at the exit, and I raced for the door.

"Stoop!" they shouted. "Vee muust talk to you!"

Part of me thought I should be polite and answer, but since you're not supposed to talk to strangers (especially if they have giant guns pointed at you), I decided it was time to get a little fresh air.

I reached the door and

K-LUNK!

opened it into my face. (Don't you hate it when that happens?)

I tried again, this time stepping back. My new approach worked brilliantly. I threw open the door and dashed outside.

"Stoop!" they shouted. "Dun't let hem geet avay!"

After the usual crashing into a half-dozen pedestrians, I was back on my feet and racing across the street for all I was worth—which, if I wasn't careful, would be about eighty-nine cents (the price of that chewing gum I'd stuffed into my pocket).

And then, if that wasn't enough . . .

"Stop! Thief!" Oh boy, a brand-new voice was added to the chaos. "Come back here with my laser vest!" It was the owner of Destructo Lasers. Apparently he wanted to join in the fun and games, too.

Yes sir, it was getting to be a real party—just like old times. Call me a Gloomy Gus (or at least a whining Wally), but for some reason I suspected I'd stepped smack-dab into another world-famous, custom-designed, patent-pending McDoogle mishap.

Chapter 2

A Scummy Swim

Yes sir, it had turned into quite the parade.

There I was in the lead, doing the usual running-for-my-life routine (not, of course, without the expected tripping and stumbling along the way).

Immediately behind me was my old buddy, Tall Guy, yelling: "Stoop, lettle boy! Vee muust talk to you!"

Next up was his partner, a charming fellow who hadn't quite mastered the fine art of sweet-talking: "Stoop or vee blow you to kingdom cume." (See what I mean?)

And finally the owner of Destructo Lasers. "Stop, thief! Stop!"

The good news was the street was pretty crowded. With any luck I could get across it and lose them. The bad news was we all know about my luck. . . .

With my incredible agility and superhuman skill
(yeah, right), I managed to dodge the first two cars.

*HONK HONK
SQUEAL! SQUEAL!*

But with my klutz-oid clumsiness and incredible
lack of coordination (that's more like it), I managed
to step right in front of a speeding motorcyclist.

*BEEP BEEP
K-THUDD!*
"Yeow!"
K-BLUB-Blub-blub . . .

If you're an experienced McDoogle reader, you've
probably figured out what the *BEEP BEEP* and
K-THUDD! were. And if you guessed that the
"Yeow" was me flying up into the air and over
the handlebars, you got that right, too. But the
K-BLUB-Blub-blub was a brand-new sound—the
sound of a thirteen-year-old boy smashing into
the chest of a very overfed biker with a long white
beard. (I don't want to say he was fat, but as I sat
on his lap I had this sudden urge to start telling
him everything I wanted for Christmas.)

But Beefy the Biker Boy had other things on his
mind—like trying to see where he was going. "Get

out of my way!" he shouted. "I can't see the road! Move it, move it!"

I tried to obey, but we were going so fast I was pinned across his front like a bug plastered to a windshield.

"Move it! Move it!"

"I'm trying! I'm trying!"

"Move it! Move it!"

"I'm trying! I'm trying!"

After a few more minutes of this stimulating conversation, I realized it was getting us nowhere. Unfortunately, I couldn't say the same thing for his driving, or lack of it. I turned my head just far enough to see that we were heading directly for the sidewalk.

"Look out!" I cried. "Turn right!"

"What?"

"Turn right, turn right!"

"Your right or mine?"

"Yours!" I shouted. "No, mine!"

"WHAT?"

"JUST TURN!"

He did. Unfortunately, it was the wrong way. Now we were swerving down the sidewalk at a gazillion miles an hour.

"EEEK! AWKK! CRY! SCREAM!"

That, of course, was the sound of pedestrians leaping for their lives.

The good news was we didn't hit a single one.

K-CLANG K-CLANG K-CLANG

The bad news was we snagged a few parking meters along the way.

But that wasn't the end of our little bumper car performance. Oh no, we were just warming up. . . .

We bounced back onto the street. Fortunately, there was no oncoming traffic. Unfortunately, it was because of the MEN WORKING sign dead ahead.

K-RASH!

Well, it had been dead ahead. Now it was sailing high into the air and joining our collection of parking meters somewhere behind us.

Next up were the little orange cones.

K-BOP K-BOP K-BOP

And finally, although Mom said never to pick up hitchhikers . . .

"AUGH!"
K-BLUB-Blub-blub . . .

Our duo had suddenly become a trio. One of the "men working" was suddenly sitting beside me on the lap of Beefy the Biker Boy.

"Hi there," I said, sticking out my hand to shake his. "My name is Wally McDoogle."

"WHAT'S GOING ON?!" he cried.

"Oh, just one of my little mishaps. Don't worry, it'll be over soon."

"WHAT?"

"I said, don't worry, these catastrophes only last a few minutes and then they'll be—" It was then I spotted the giant open manhole we were approaching. "See," I said, calmly pointing. "It's just like I said. It'll all be over in a . . . AUGHhhhh!"

K-SPLASH!
glug-glug-glug-glug . . .

I would have continued chatting, but it can be hard keeping up a conversation when you're busy drowning in a city storm drain.

It's not that I'm a bad swimmer. It's just that I have this thing about staying on top of water.

I don't.

I also have this thing about panicking and breathing under water.

I do. A lot.

So there I was swimming like an Olympic gold

medal rock, when suddenly I noticed there was something moving in my pocket.

Something alive!

At first I thought it might be a lizard or a fish that had squirmed in. But then I noticed something else—it was growing! Fast! Almost as fast as the interest on Mom's credit cards.

It burst through my pocket and continued to grow. And then I recognized it. It was a package of chewing gum! The one the blond guy at Destructo Lasers had given me!

And it was still growing!

Now it was the size of a loaf of bread . . . then a breadbox . . . then a bread truck!

As it grew, it began to take shape. It began looking like a lifeboat. In a flash of genius my superior intellect figured out the reason—it *was* a lifeboat! One of those inflatable kind—complete with inflatable oars, inflatable life vests, and the ever-popular inflatable TV and VCR (obviously for longer cruises).

The boat shot to the surface, and I quickly climbed into it.

That was the good news. But, as you might have guessed, there was some bad news.

The current on the surface was strong in a major white-water-rafting kind of way. In fact, the boat and I were flying through the storm drain faster

than Dad drives on vacation when he thinks Mom
has fallen asleep beside him.

I knew the time had finally come. It was time
for me to suck it in and do what I do best. It was
time for me to open my mouth and scream:

"SOMEBODY HELP ME!!!"

But there were no somebodies around—not even
Beefy the Biker Boy or my construction buddy.
Just me, this weird lifeboat, and the oars. (I would
have mentioned the TV and VCR, but I couldn't
find the remote, so what good were they?)

It was about this time that I saw a little speck of
daylight ahead. A little speck that was quickly turning into a larger dot, that was quickly turning into
an even larger circle. All right! I was coming out of
the storm drain!

I grabbed the oars and began rowing, trying to
stay in the center of the giant pipe. The light grew
bigger and bigger, the opening wider and wider.
Finally I shot out of the pipe, into the open air,
and—

"Uh-oh."

I glanced down and saw the Middleton River
a mere seventy-five feet below.

Seventy-five FEET!?

I quickly grabbed the oars and began rowing

like I'd never rowed before. But oars don't work that well in midair. So, once again, I began my falling-like-a-rock routine. And, once again, I did what I do best:

"AUGHHHHHhhhh . . ."

We hit the water hard.

KER-SPLASH

In fact, we hit so hard that I bounced out of the boat and was once again airborne—which, of course, meant a repeat in the

"AUGHHHHHhhhh . . ."

department. But a moment later I crashed into the soft, sandy shore.

K-SMOOPH

As I lay there, trying to regain consciousness, I was a little disappointed. I mean, I could have brought a beach towel and some suntan lotion— you know, to try to tone up my tan a little before dying. After all, it's important to look your best for those morgue photos.

Unfortunately, my little stroll through Weirdville hadn't exactly come to an end. Not yet.

"Zer hee iz!"

I raised my head from the sand and saw my favorite tall bad guy racing down the riverbank after me. And just behind him was his short buddy, Mr. Sweet Talker himself, yelling, "Stoop or I vill blow you to kingdom cume!"

And behind him?

"Stop, thief, stop!"

It was kinda nice to see the old gang together again. But as much as I wanted to stick around and catch up on old times, there was something inside me that thought living might be a better idea. So I leaped to my feet and quickly

K- Smooph!

fell over a piece of driftwood.

I jumped up and started running again. I noticed a highway following the river so I headed toward it. If I could reach it and flag down a passing car—

"Stoop, lettle boy, vee muust talk to you!"

I was closing in on the road. It was forty feet ahead . . . thirty . . . twenty . . . but my bad boy buddies were closing in faster.

"Stoop or vee vill blow you to kingdom cume!"

And then I saw it . . . coming down the road. An

approaching van. I waved my arms wildly and shouted at the top of my lungs. "Help me! You've got to help me!"

Now the road was fifteen feet away . . . ten . . .

"Stoop, little boy, vee muust talk to you!"

I threw a look over my shoulder. Tall Guy was just a few steps behind. "Help me!" I shouted at the van. "Help!"

I reached the road and began running alongside of it. "Help me!"

The van slowed and eased up beside me.

"Help me!"

"Stoop, . . . lettle boy!" Tall Guy was reaching out. He nearly had me.

Suddenly the side door to the van slid open. Inside was a kindly looking man in some sort of paramilitary uniform. "Jump!" he shouted as he motioned with his hands. "Jump, Wally! Jump!"

I wasn't sure who he was, or how he knew my name, but—

"Stoop, lettle boy!"

I didn't think now was the time to play twenty questions. I veered toward the van and reached out to the military guy. He reached out to me.

We were just about to grab each other when Tall Guy suddenly felt this urge to leap into the air and grab me around the waist. He got me, and we both fell to the ground.

"OAFF!"

I looked up as the van raced away. "Don't leave me!" I cried. "Don't leave!" But the driver didn't seem to be in a listening mood.

I rolled to my side and broke free of Tall Guy just long enough to get to my feet and take off.

"Stoop or I vill blow you to kingdom cume!"

Ah, yes, I'd almost forgotten. Sweet-talking Short Stuff was still behind me. And by the sound of things, it was his turn to be closing in.

Suddenly, there was a loud squeal. I looked up to see that the van had turned and slammed on its brakes. Now it was parked directly in front of me, less than twenty feet away. The military guy motioned toward me and shouted, "Hurry!"

I hurried.

Behind me, I could hear Tall Guy scrambling back to his feet. "Vee muust talk! Vee muust talk!"

"Hurry, Wally! Hurry!"

I was fifteen feet from the van . . . ten . . .

Short Stuff continued closing in. "Stoop or I vill blow you to kingdom cume!"

And what party would be complete without the Destructo Lasers owner?

"Stop, thief! Stop!"

Yes sir, all of my friends were there. And they were all gaining on me.

I was five feet from the van.

"Jump!" the military guy shouted. "Jump!"

I nodded and with all of my strength leaped toward the van's open door—just as it peeled out and zoomed away . . . *without me!*

WHAT?

There I was, sailing through the air toward the . . . well, toward nothing. A moment ago I had been heading toward an open van. Now there was nothing in front of me but thin air—and a wheelchair.

A WHEELCHAIR!!?

That's right.

For some unexplained reason, somebody had parked an empty wheelchair right behind the van. So, instead of hitting the ground face first, I hit the wheelchair face first. That was the good news. Unfortunately, there were a couple of pieces of bad news:

Bad News #1—That same somebody had not bothered to set the wheelchair's brakes.

Bad News #2—The wheelchair was parked at the top of a very steep slope.

Well, it had been parked at the top of a very steep slope. Now it was rolling down that very steep slope with one very reluctant passenger clinging to it and screaming for his life.

"AUGHhhh . . ."

Faster and faster I rolled. There was no way to steer the thing and no way to stop it. But that was the least of my worries because straight ahead I noticed a slightly bigger one.

Directly in front of me a huge building towered at the end of the street. The very street I was currently setting the world's land speed record on.

"AUGHhhh . . ." x 2

After another prayer (where I promised God not only to empty that garbage but the cat box as well), I braced myself for the worst.

But the worst never happened.

Instead, it was worse than the worst. Just before I hit the building, the front door miraculously slid open and I rolled inside—past the waiting area, past the receptionist's desk, and directly into a . . . *K-POOF!* . . . wall.

But this was no ordinary wall. Instead of plaster or wood or some other bone-breaking hardness, it was made of extra-thick foam padding. A padding that caught me like a giant feather bed.

Suddenly everything was silent. No screaming Tall Guy, no screaming Short Stuff—and, most importantly, no screaming Wally.

After a long moment of catching my breath, I finally reached down and rolled the wheelchair and myself out of the wall. For the most part, nothing was too badly broken. For that I was relieved. Until I heard a voice behind me—

"Good evening, Mr. McDoogle."

I froze. There was something strangely familiar about that voice. Something about the thick English accent that I recognized.

Slowly, I turned to see . . .

It was the blond guy. The man they shot back at Destructo Lasers. The one who had died right in front of my eyes. Only now he was sitting in a fancy chair, behind a desk, wearing a fancy three-piece suit, and, most importantly, there were no longer any fancy bullet holes filling his body.

He smiled. "Nice to see you again, Wallace."

Chapter 3

Spy Guy

So there I was, staring at a man who was supposed to have stopped breathing in a major kind of way. I opened my mouth and in my coolest, most casual voice said:

"B . . . b . . . bu . . . but . . ."

He smiled again.

I continued displaying my incredible speaking ability: "You're . . . you're . . . you're . . . you're . . ."

"I'm supposed to be dead?" he asked.

I nodded, grateful for the help.

"Yes," he said, "that's what they're supposed to think."

"They?"

He nodded and reached to a computer keyboard on his desk. He hit a few keys and suddenly

G-zzzzz . . .

a glass wall slid across the doorway I'd entered—
just as Tall Guy and his pal, Short Stuff, arrived.

They didn't look too happy about the situation.
In fact, once they arrived, they began banging on
the glass and shouting all sorts of "you-can't-say-
that-in-Sunday-school" kinda stuff.

For some reason it didn't look like they could
see us. But we could sure see and hear them. And
the more I saw and heard, the more nervous I
got.

"Not to worry," the man behind the desk
chuckled. "It's a steel-reinforced, one-way mirror.
They can't see us, and they can't break through."

"But . . . but . . . who are they?" I croaked. "And
. . . *who are you?*"

He rose up from his desk and stuck out his
hand. "The name is Blond . . . James Blond. I work
for Her Majesty's Central Security Agency."

I reached across his desk to shake his hand but
accidentally knocked over a family photo instead.
No problem . . . except the photo toppled into his
pencil holder . . . which knocked into his cup of tea
. . . which spilled out across his desk into all sorts
of electronic gizmos and doodads.

> *CRACKLE . . . CRACKLE*
> *SPARK . . . SPARK*
> *SIZZLE . . . SIZZLE*

Mr. Blond could only stare in astonishment as the smoke slowly rose from his desk. "Amazing," he whispered in awe, "simply amazing."

"I'm . . . I'm sorry," I stuttered.

"Nothing to worry about, old chap," he said as he continued to stare and shake his head. "Our intelligence report said this sort of thing always happens to you, but I had to see it to believe it."

"Your *'intelligence report'*?" I asked.

"Yes. Ever since our little run-in at Destructo Lasers, we've been—"

"Hey, I didn't do it," I interrupted. "It wasn't my fault."

He looked at me and let out a quiet sigh. "The report said you'd say that as well."

"What do you mean?"

"Apparently, you are the type who doesn't take responsibility for your actions."

"I am?"

"If you would have taken responsibility for causing me to fall, if you would have told those gentlemen that it was simply an accident, they may have believed you. But when you denied it, and when they heard us talking, they naturally figured we worked together."

"You mean," I tried to swallow back the lump growing in my throat, "they think I'm a secret agent, too?"

"Precisely."

"Oh boy!"

"And now, in a sense, you are."

"I am?"

"We suspect there is a leak in our security. It's imperative that everyone inside the intelligence community including our friends out there"—he motioned toward my buddies who were still banging on the mirror—"it's imperative that they all think I'm dead."

I frowned. "Why?"

"They overheard us talking. They know I told you the location of the Giggle Gun."

"Giggle Gun?" I exclaimed. "There really is such a thing?"

"Oh yes. And it really is in a cave in Africa." He took a deep breath and slowly let it out. "And now I'm afraid you must go to Africa in my place and pretend to search for it."

"You're kidding?"

"Central Security Agents never kid. Your father is already en route to join us and—"

"Dad?"

"Correct."

"My dad's coming *here?*"

"Why does that surprise you? The fate of the entire free world depends upon the success of this operation."

"I know, but . . ."

"But what?"

"Well, it's *Monday Night Football.*"

Mr. Blond blinked.

I tried to smile.

He blinked again. Obviously, he didn't know how important football was to Dad. He cleared his throat and continued. "You must hurry. You have less than one hour to wash up and prepare for your flight."

"Flight?"

"As I said, it's important that you appear to carry on the mission."

"But . . . but . . . but," I was starting my motorboat imitation again. "I can't carry out any mission."

"Of course you can, Wallace. You've already passed our tests."

"Tests?"

"You expertly rode with our agent on the motorcycle."

"That was one of your guys?"

"Certainly. And you handled yourself excellently in the storm drain, deployed the lifeboat, navigated the pipe, and landed on the beach, exactly as we had planned."

"You planned all of that?"

He nodded. "Just as we planned the van, the

wheelchair, and your dropping in here for our little visit."

I couldn't find my voice. (It's hard to talk when you're in major shock.)

"Now, if you'll head on into the next room over there."

He hit some more computer keys and the back wall of the room slid open. Amazing. On the other side was a mini-hotel room complete with shower and a fresh change of clothes on the bed—clothes exactly like I would wear. But that wasn't my only surprise. . . . On a little coffee table sat an exact replica of Ol' Betsy, my laptop computer!

"Wow," I cried, "you guys thought of everything!"

"That's why they pay us the big, spy-guy bucks."

I turned to him and scowled. "But I've still got one question."

"Yes."

"Back at Destructo Lasers . . . I mean, after they were done shooting, you should have had more holes in you than a piece of Swiss cheese."

He rose to his feet and smiled. "Actually, Wallace, I wasn't at Destructo Lasers."

"Of course you were."

"No, that was just a 3-D holographic image."

If my jaw had dropped any lower, they'd have had to dig it out of the floor. "You were there," I said. "I saw you!"

"You only thought you did."

"But . . . you looked so . . . real!"

"As real as I do now?"

"Absolutely."

He nodded and reached down to his computer keyboard. "Well, don't believe everything you see, Wallace." With that he hit three keys. And suddenly, his image and the keyboard itself began to waver.

"Hey!" I shouted.

Then they started to disappear.

"What are you doing?" I cried. "You can't go!"

"The limo will be here with your father in exactly fifty-three minutes. Good luck, Agent 00½th. And remember, the fate of the entire free world lies in your hands."

"But . . ."

"Good evening."

"But . . . but . . ."

But there were no more buts. He was gone. Disappeared. Vanished as completely as if he had never been there. And the reason was pretty simple—he never had been.

* * * * *

The clothes were a perfect fit, just like the ones back home. But without all the rips, patches, and bloodstains from past McDoogle mishaps. (These spy guys may be good, but they're not that good.)

The replica of Ol' Betsy was practically the same, too. I flipped her on and checked some of my files. Sure enough, they'd even entered my old superhero stories. There were Mutant Man McDoogle, Gnat Man, Hydro Dude, Floss Man, Tidy Guy, Bumble Boy, and more. They were all there, and it was pretty impressive.

I had a half-hour to kill before Dad and the limo showed up. I hoped he would explain more of what was going on. Until then, I did what I always do to unwind—I sat down and started another one of my stories. But I wanted this one to be different. I wanted it to be calm and peaceful—not at all like the crazy dream (or was it a nightmare?) I was currently living.

It is a nice afternoon in Niceville. The sun is shining nicely, the birds are twittering nicely, and the children are playing (what else, but)... nicely. In fact, it's so nice that our world-famous superhero and computer-generated character, Gigabyte Guy, decides to take the rest of the day off.

Just a few hours earlier he had cured
a hundred computer viruses, deleted a
thousand junk e-mails, and shut down
an Internet server that was busy every
time you tried to dial up.

Now he is looking forward to kick-
ing back, munching on a nice bowl of
megabytes (even though he is putting
on some weight around the ol' hard
drive), and watching some Monday Night
Nintendo.

Before settling in, he strolls across
his desktop page to check it out. It's
exactly as he suspects, everything is
...nice.

He checks out his CD-ROM. It's also
...nice.

The same goes for his Web site.

Yes sir, everything's just the way he
likes it, nice and, well,...nice.

"Excuse me?"

He wanders into his nicely deco-
rated kitchen and pours himself a nice
glass of—

"Excuse me, Mr. Wally?"

I stopped writing. It was happening again. One of my characters was talking back to me. I tried to ignore him, but it did no good.

"Excuse me, Mr. Wally? It's Gigabyte Guy."

Reluctantly, I typed, **"Yes?"**

"Listen, I know you've had a stressed-out day and all, but..."

"But what?" I typed.

"Well, why do you have to take it out on me?"

I frowned at the screen, then typed, **"Take what out on you? What are you talking about?"**

"No offense, but this is the most boring story you've ever written."

I typed back, **"It's supposed to help me relax."**

"But I'm a superhero. Superheroes are supposed to live superhero lives—you know, with superhero suspense and superhero action (and a little superhero romance wouldn't hurt either)."

"This is a kid's story," I typed. **"Who wants all that huggy-kissy stuff?"**

He shrugged. "Yeah, you're right. But what about the superhero action and superhero suspense?"

"What's wrong with just having a nice day?" I typed.

"It's not fair. All your other super-heroes got to do superhero stuff. Ecology Man got to fight Toxoid Breath. Neutron Dude got to fight Veggie Man. Even Floss Man, who I thought was the lamest superhero of all, got to battle it out with Harry the Hairball."

"So?"

"So, all you've got me doing is sit-ting around and watching NTV?"

I saw his point. And as much as I hated to do it (you give made-up characters an inch and they'll take a mile), I typed, "So do you have any suggestions?"

"Hey, that's your job!" he complained. "I'm the superhero. You're the writer!"

"All right, all right," I typed, "don't get your A drive in a bunch." I scowled hard, thinking over the last few hours. What would be a good bad thing for Gigabyte Guy to stop? Suddenly, I snapped my fingers. "I've got it!"

"Are you sure?" he asked. "It's not going to be some loser thing like, 'Suddenly his computer screen gets dust on it,' is it?"

"No way," I typed. "This is going to be great." Before he could do any more complaining, I went back to my story.

Suddenly, Gigabyte's monitor gives a little shudder. He strolls to the edge of his screen, looks out, and sees that a baseball has gently rolled against it. A sweet little boy skips merrily into the room to retrieve it, and——"
"Boring, boring, boring..."
"Sorry," I typed. I hit delete and tried again.

Suddenly Gigabyte's monitor shatters into a thousand pieces! He races to the edge of the screen and spots an inner-city gang member storming into the room after his baseball. Along with him comes his international-terrorist brother and escaped-convict father.
"Look what you've done to my screen!" Gigabyte cries.
"It's not my fault!" the kid yells, as he grabs the baseball. "Blame my brother for making me play with him!"
"It's not my fault!" the brother yells. "Blame my dad for giving me the ball!"

"It's not my fault!" Dad cries. "Blame the warden for letting me steal it out of his office!"

Gigabyte frowns. Something is weird in *The Twilight Zone* kind of way. Suddenly his e-mail flashes. He punches it up to see the President of the United States on the screen. "Gigabyte Guy!" he calls. "Where are you?"

"Right in front of you, sir."

"Well, it's not my fault I can't see you. It's these stupid glasses."

"Yes, sir."

"And it's not my fault they're stupid. Blame my eye doctor."

"Yes, sir."

"And don't blame me for choosing the eye doctor, blame the person who——"

"Mr. President," Gigabyte interrupts, "What are you saying?"

"It's not my fault that you don't know."

"Mr. President, nobody is blaming you for anything."

"Well, don't blame me for that, either!"

Before any more excuses can be made, the President's image breaks up and dissolves into another——

"Good evening, Geeko Guy."

Our superhero gasps a superhero breath. There, on the screen before him, is the dreaded and definitely not-so-nice (insert bad guy music here) Excuso Man.

"Excuso Man!" our hero gasps. "I might have guessed. You're the reason everyone is making excuses!"

Suddenly the sinister sinner sneers a sinisterly snide sneer. (I hope you're not having to read this out loud.) "Very good, Geeko Guy."

"But how...why?"

The villainous villain steps back to reveal a giant cannon pointed toward the sky. "Behold...my latest weapon."

"What is it?"

"The Excuse-a-tron."

"The Excuse-a-tron! Wasn't that Proverb Guy's weapon way back in book six?!"

"Bingo!" The bad-breathed bad boy barks. "But your pal, the author there, never destroyed it. So I've swiped it and reversed the effects. Now, instead of stealing excuses from people, it's flooding the world with them."

"You don't mean——"

"That's right. As I release its rays into the atmosphere, our entire world is filling with *ir*-responsibility. Soon no one will take responsibility for anything again. They will always have an excuse. They will always blame somebody else."

"Hey, Mr. Wally!"

It was Gigabyte Guy again.

"That's pretty good."

"Thanks," I typed, "but if you keep interrupting, we'll never get on with the story."

"Oh, sorry. What am I going to do now?"

"Just be patient." I went back to typing.

"Oh no!" our superhero cries. "Alack and forsooth!"

"Alack and forsooth!?" It was Gigabyte again. "No one ever says 'Alack and forsooth!'" (See what I mean about giving these characters an inch?) "Why not have me say——"

Honk Honk

I looked up from Ol' Betsy and saw a limo the size of Cleveland pulling up outside my window.

Honk Honk

I would have loved to have finished arguing with Giga Guy. Better yet, I would have loved to have finished my story. But at the moment there were a few other details to take care of.

I shut down Ol' Betsy, grabbed my coat, and headed out the door. Sometimes, saving the world can be a real nuisance. But a guy's gotta do what a guy's gotta do.

Chapter 4

The Gang's All Here

The chauffeur opened the limo door, and I stepped inside.

"Hey, Wally!"

I looked down to the far end of the car and saw Wall Street. She was sitting at a computer screen doing what she did best—watching the latest stock reports. (Wall Street has this thing about making money.)

"What are you doing here?" I asked. But before she could answer, I heard another familiar sound.

K-RUNCH K-RUNCH K-RUNCH

I spun around to see my other best friend, Opera, doing what he did best—inhaling his third bag of Chippy Chipper Potato Chips. (Opera has this thing about junk food.)

And just behind Opera, glued to the big screen TV (hey, it's a long limo), was my dad.

"Pass interference?! You're crazy! He didn't touch the guy!"

"Hi, Dad."

No answer.

"Dad?"

Ditto in the no answer department.

"He's kinda involved in the game," Wall Street whispered.

I nodded. We may have been out to save the world, but it *was still Monday Night Football.*

"Why are you guys here?" I asked, as the limo lurched forward and we started toward the airport. "Did they tell you what's going on?"

Wall Street answered. "They said you hurt some government guy and now you have to do his job."

"That's it?" I asked.

Opera nodded and, with a mouthful of chips, added, "Mand mou may mou're mot memofmobile . . . Burp."

(Translation: *"And you say you're not responsible . . . Burp."*)

Having been best friends forever, I understood him perfectly. "It's true," I insisted, "I'm *not* responsible!"

Wall Street nodded. "Yeah, they said you'd say that."

"But I'm not!"

"They said you'd say that, too. Anyway," Wall Street continued, "they thought you'd like some company, so here we are."

"You guys would do this for me?" I asked.

"Sure," Wall Street grinned. "Well, for you and for all the cool stuff they're giving us."

"Stuff?"

"You know . . . the digital TV, the monster sound system, and all the videos and CDs we want."

"You're letting them bribe you?!"

"Sure."

"I can't believe you're that shallow, that you could be bought so cheaply."

"Yeah," Opera agreed, finally coming up for air. "At least I held out for a lifetime supply of potato *Belch!* chips."

"Don't worry, Wally," Wall Street said. "They didn't forget you."

"Mhat's miight," Opera said, cramming a fresh supply of chips into his mouth. He reached over and plopped a little shaving kit on my lap.

I looked down at it. "A shaving bag? They gave me a shaving bag?"

"It's not just a bag," Wall Street laughed. "Open it."

I did.

"See?" she continued, doing her best to sound cheery. "There's all kinds of stuff inside. A nice toothbrush, here's some toothpaste, oh, and here's a nice pair of toenail clippers. I think they're Swiss army," she said even more cheerfully.

"Terrific," I sighed. "They've got me risking my life for a set of toenail clippers."

Suddenly Opera's nonstop crunching stopped.

So did Wall Street's nonstop cheeriness.

"What's wrong?" I asked.

"Did you say . . ." Wall Street took a breath, *"risking your life?"*

"Of course. Didn't they tell you how dangerous this would be?"

She shook her head. "They just said we'd be taking a free trip around the world with you."

I looked at them. They looked at me. Finally, Opera said what we all were thinking:

"Muh-moh . . ."

But before anyone could respond, the limo swerved hard to the left, and we flew across the car. I shouted, Wall Street screamed, and Opera belched.

Even Dad managed to glance up from the game just long enough to yell, "Hey, you're spilling my soda!"

But that was only the beginning. Suddenly our car picked up speed—a lot of it. We took another hard left and then a right.

"What's going on?" Wall Street cried.

I raced to the back of the limo and looked out the rear window. We were zipping by all the cars like they were standing still. Well, all the cars but one—the one that was right on our tail. The one that veered hard to the left when we veered hard to the left . . . and veered hard to the right when we veered hard to the right.

I yelled over my shoulder, "I think we've got company!"

"They better have brought their own food!" Dad shouted.

Without warning, the limo suddenly spun into a 180-degree turn as we resumed our chorus of shouting, screaming, and belching. I wound up smashed against the side window and managed to look out just in time to see the other car zooming past. Sure enough, there were my old pals, Tall Guy and Short Stuff.

After the limo made a few more *s*werves, *s*kids, and *s*queals (accompanied by our *s*houts, *s*hrieks, and *s*creams), we finally got to hear a new "s" sound.

SCREECH!

The car stopped suddenly, and we flew forward.

SMASH!
(Oh boy, another new "s" word!)

With our faces scrunched against the front glass we could see the airport. But that wasn't all we saw.

"Say, Dad?"

"Yes, Son."

"How come our chauffeur is running away from the car as fast as he can?"

"Got me," Dad shrugged. "It probably has something to do with those guys who are chasing us—you know, the ones who are trying to kill us."

We all looked at each other and then, in perfect unison, cried:

"TRYING TO KILL US!?"

"What do we do?" Wall Street screamed.

"Met's met mout mof mhere!"

I couldn't agree with Opera more. I slid across the seat and pushed at the door.

Nothing.

I pushed harder.

Double nothing.

"We're trapped!" I cried. "Like fish in a barrel!"

"Like rats in a trap!" Wall Street screamed.

"Like going to the movies without money for popcorn!" (Apparently Opera had finished his chips.)

I leaned back and slammed into the door with all my might.

K-CRACK

Something gave way. Unfortunately, that something had nothing to do with the door—and everything to do with my body.

"Oww," I groaned, "my shoulder."

"Hurry!" Wall Street screamed. "Hurry!"

"Uh, Wally?" Dad asked.

"Not now, Dad, I have to save our lives." I leaned back and hit the door even harder.

K-CRACK!

Double the volume, double the pain.

Things were getting desperate. Not only had I run out of shoulders to break, but the bad guys would be there any minute.

"Uh, Wally?"

"Dad, not now."

I leaned back a third time and hit the door for all I was worth.

K-SMUSH!
*(That's the sound bodies make when there
are no more bones left to break.)*

"Wally?"

I love my dad, but he was really getting on my nerves. "What do you want?" I demanded.

"Maybe if you unlocked it first?"

I glanced up to the lock. "Oh." (Don't parents ever get tired of being right?) I yanked up the lock and the door popped open.

"Thanks!" I cried as I grabbed my stuff and tumbled out of the car onto the pavement.

"Don't mention it," he said tumbling out right on top of me. (And they say clumsiness isn't genetic.)

As we struggled to our feet, a car's headlights blinded us as it sped around the corner.

"Oh, no!" Wall Street cried. "What do we do?"

I looked at Dad.

Dad looked at me.

We both had the same answer:

"RUN!!!"

Chapter 5

Mush, Fido, Mush!

Opera and Wall Street took off toward the airport.
Dad and I were right behind—well, except for the
part where we ran into each other.

K-THUDD!!

Like father, like son.

By the time we pulled ourselves up off of each
other, my bad boy buddies were leaping out of
their car and racing toward us while doing their
usual shouting routine:

"Vee muust talk. . . . Stoop or I vill blow you to
kingdom cume!"

We took off running without bothering to look
behind. Unfortunately, we didn't seem to be looking
ahead too well either.

K-RASH!
roll . . . roll . . . roll . . . roll . . .

We hit a stray luggage cart and began rolling down the sidewalk at just under 1.2 billion miles an hour.

"AUGH!"
"AUGHhhh!"

We were both screaming and lying spread-eagle across the cart—Dad on the top, me on the bottom. I was about to mention how nice it was to finally share a father and son moment (and that we'd finally found a hobby we could both enjoy) when I happened to glance up and see Opera and Wall Street straight ahead.

"Look out!" I cried. "Look out!"

The good news was they spotted us coming. The bad news was it was too late.

K-THUDD! K-THUDD!

Our little duet had now become a quartet. And, for the most part, our harmony was pretty good:

"AUGH!"
"AUGHhhh!"
"AUGHhhhhhh!"
"AUGHhhhhhhhh!"

But before we had a chance to audition for any recording contracts (or at least lay down a hat for people to drop spare change into), we picked up a fifth member of the act.

K-POW!

It was a giant pet cage.

The impact was so great that it knocked open the cage door, and a pet the size of Seattle bolted out. I couldn't tell if it was a Great Dane or a baby elephant . . . until he began to bark.

WOOF! WOOF! WOOF!

The sound was so loud that it hurt my ears. But that was nothing compared to the pain the rest of my body would soon be in. Because as Fido—the Monster Dog—began to bark, he also began to run.

Normally this wouldn't be a problem, except that his leash was tangled around the front of our luggage cart. So the faster he ran, the faster we rolled.

"Look out!" I shouted.

WOOF!

"Coming through!"

WOOF! WOOF!

So there I was doing a dogsled imitation through
the airport as all sorts of folks leaped out of the
way. With a little bit of strain and a lot of stretch-
ing, I reached forward to the leash. I tried my best
to untangle the knot, but the harder Fido pulled,
the tighter it got.

"Do something!" Wall Street yelled.

"Like what?" I cried.

"Like anything!"

Actually, I figured I'd done enough already. With
all the trouble I'd gone to to get us into this mess,
I figured it was only fair that somebody else get
us out. And since Dad was the designated grownup
of the group, I turned to him for help.

"You have to cut the leash!" he shouted.

"With what?" I yelled. "I don't have anything
but this shaving kit."

"Look inside! There must be something!"

I opened the kit and shook my head. "There's just
this toothbrush, toothpaste, and nail clippers—"

"That's it!" he shouted. "Use the nail clippers!"

I pulled out the clippers, and after the usual fum-
bling, I managed to get them open. Then, reaching out to the leash, I began cutting away.

I was amazed at how sharp the clippers were
(superspies must have supertough toenails). In a
matter of seconds the leash snapped. Ol' Fido
broke free and ran off to share his terror with the

rest of the airport—which was okay by me because as I glanced up, I saw we'd soon be experiencing plenty of terror on our own.

Directly in front of us was a moving escalator!

"AUGH!"
SWOOSH
BANG BANG BANG BANG

Well, it had been in front of us. Now we were busy bouncing down its stairs.

"W-w-w-will . . . s-s-s-ome-b-b-body . . . t-t-t-urn . . . this-is-is . . . th-th-thing . . . of-f-f-f-f!?" I cried.

But my buddies were too busy screaming their own lungs out to pay attention. The ride seemed to go on forever—and for good reason.

It was.

We were bouncing down an UP escalator. As we kept rolling down and down and down, the stairs kept coming up and up and up. It was like one of those perpetual motion machines, never stopping.

We would be there to this day if it weren't for that poor little man with the cane who didn't bother to look up before he stepped on.

"Look out!" I shouted. "Mister, look—"

K-BLAMB

"YEOWwwwwww . . ."

"Sorry . . ." I shouted as he flew high over our heads.

Fortunately, the little collision knocked over our cart and we tumbled out. For a moment we lay there, sprawling this way and that, as the moving stairs carried us back toward the top.

Unfortunately, when we arrived there was a welcoming party waiting for us.

"Good effening. It'z zo nize of you to stoop by and—" But that was all my bad guy buddies got out before

". . . wwwwwwAAHH!"

Flying Gramps with the cane landed

K-SMASH!

smack dab on top of them.

We reached the top of the stairs and scrambled to our feet. Unfortunately, the bad guys were also scrambling to theirs.

"Run!" Dad shouted. "I'll hold them off. Run!"

"But—"

"Run, Wally! Run!"

I tell you, just when you think you've got your

parents figured out, just when you're sure the only reason they had you was so they could get a tax deduction, they go and pull something like this. Don't get me wrong, I know my dad loves me. But as a man's man he doesn't go out of his way to say it. Still, when the chips are down, there he was ready, willing, and—

"Wally, will you quit jabbering and get your rear in gear!"

See what I mean? I nodded and the three of us took off faster than a kid who'd drunk too much prune juice.

But not fast enough.

BEEP BEEP
K-BAMB!

Suddenly we found ourselves the hood ornament to one of those golf-cart-like people transporters.

"Move it!" the driver shouted. "I can't see! Move it! Move it!"

I looked up, and there was my old pal, Beefy the Biker Boy—all three thousand pounds of him. I wanted to ask how'd he been, maybe check out the latest pictures of his kids, but he was too busy trying to see where he was going.

"Move it! Move it! Move it!"

Yes sir, it was just like old times.

BEEP BEEP BEEP BEEP

Once again, people were screaming and leaping out of the way. Once again, we were swerving wildly out of control.

We zipped by the ticket line.

"Look out!"

Past the ticket agent.

"Coming through!"

And entered the long Jetway. For a moment everything appeared to be settling down until

K-THUNK

we hit the doorway of the plane. Fortunately, the golf cart was too big to get inside and came to a sudden halt. Unfortunately, we weren't and didn't. The three of us flew into the plane and

K-THUDD

hit the opposite wall.

For a moment I lay there on my back sort of dazed. Then, when I finally started to move, checking for missing or broken body parts, I heard an all too familiar voice.

"Good evening, Wallace. You really are quite good at this catastrophe business, aren't you?"

I looked up and, sure enough, there was James Blond sitting in a humongous leather chair, checking his watch.

"And, as always, you're right on time."

* * * * *

The plane was fixed up to look like a fancy condo, complete with kitchen, living room, and entertainment center. It was pretty cool (although I thought the hot tub and racquetball court in the back were a bit much).

After Mr. Blond promised me a hundred times that Dad would be okay and that the bad guys were after me, not him, I tried to relax. It might have been easier if I weren't so scared of heights. (As you may remember, I'm the one who gets dizzy just stepping up onto street curbs.) I had to find something to take my mind off the flying.

"Moo mome mritting," Opera suggested as he buckled in beside me.

(Obviously he'd found their stash of chips in the kitchen.)

"How can I 'do some writing'?" I complained. "I don't even have Ol' Betsy."

"Mhat's mat?" he pointed.

I looked over to a nearby table. Sure enough, there was another laptop exactly like the other Ol' Betsy.

"These guys are good," I marveled.

"Mhey mure mare," Opera agreed as he crammed another half bag of the deep-fried, empty carbos into his mouth.

I reached for Ol' Betsy III and snapped her on. It would be several hours before we landed in Africa, and Opera was right. There's nothing like a good, danger-filled fantasy to take your mind off your own danger-filled reality.

When we last left Gigabyte Guy, he'd just learned that the entire world was being bathed in the dreaded (and not all that easy to pronounce) Irresponsible Beam. Every human on the planet was being filled with more excuses than a kid who didn't do his homework. No one was taking responsibility for anything.

Fortunately, since he's not human, the beam has no effect upon our hero's magnificent microchip mind. No wonder the President had called him. He's the only one who can save the world!

Giga Guy races to the edge of his monitor screen and starts to leap out when

K-LUNK

he hits the glass.

"Oh, that's right," he says, slapping his forehead. "I'm a computer character. I live *inside* computers." (Hey, just 'cause he's created by a computer doesn't mean he's as smart as a computer.)

"I heard that, Mr. Wally!"

Oh boy, he's trying to talk to me again. I pretended to ignore him and typed faster.

Gigabyte Guy turns from the monitor and surges through the computer's printed circuits. Grabbing his virtual reality coat and slipping on his virtual reality galoshes (How else is he going to stop from catching a virtual reality virus?), our hero prepares to exit through his modem when suddenly—

"Greetings, earthling."

He comes byte to byte with a strange character from an even stranger computer game—but not just any strange computer game. This is from the one and only (insert spooky *X-Files* music here)

ALIEN ENCOUNTER!

But how did the game get on our
hero's computer? His owner's mother
never lets him buy computer games—
unless they're the educational kind.
And from the looks of things, this bug-
eyed alien isn't your average talking
purple dinosaur trying to teach the
ABCs. In fact, this alien doesn't look
like he's interested in teaching anyone anything—unless it's a close-up
examination of his razor sharp teeth
and the inner workings of his diges-
tive system.

Gigabyte Guy leaps to the left.

But ol' Bug Eye blocks his path.

He leaps to the right.

Bug Eye's path-blocking program
repeats itself. Then, with a terrify-
ing and somewhat irritating electronic
laugh, the creature cries, "Prepare to
die, earthling."

Bug Eye approaches and Gigabyte Guy
braces himself for the worst.

Closer and closer it comes. Wider and
wider it opens its mouth. Holy hard
drive, what will our hero do? It's

hideous. Horrendous. Horrifying. But
that's enough about Bug Eye's breath.
Let's get back to Gigabyte's future—
or lack of it. In a matter of seconds,
his delete button will be hit. He'll be
clicked and pointed to the nearest
recycle bin, a soon-to-be-forgotten
blip on the printed circuits of life.

And then, just when the computer
analogies are wearing thin...

Our plane gave a sudden jerk. And then another.

I looked up from the computer. "What's that?"

Wall Street glanced from her newspaper and
looked out the window. "Uh-oh."

There was another jerk.

"What's wrong?" I asked.

"Looks like we've got company."

"Company?!"

Another jerk.

"Yeah, it's the old, midair docking routine. They
do it in all the movies now."

"Who's doing it?!"

"Let's see . . . oh, there's your father."

"My dad?!"

Wall Street nodded. "And your two buddies
from the airport, and their two guns—or are

those missile launchers? It's kinda hard to tell
from this angle. Oh, and there's—"

Suddenly a deafening hiss filled the cabin.

"What's happening!?" I cried.

"They've broken the seal!" Mr. Blond shouted
as he raced toward the front of the plane. "We're
losing cabin pressure! Buckle in kids, looks like
our little picnic is over."

Picnic?! If he thought this had been a picnic, I'd
hate to see his version of ants. But, of course, I
would, soon enough.

He turned to me and shouted, "Wally, do you
have that shaving kit we gave you?"

"Right here!" I yelled.

"Good. Get ready to use it!"

"But I'm too young to shave!" I shouted.

"Just get ready!"

Chapter 6

Midair Detour

The air continued hissing out of the cabin. Don't
get me wrong, I like a gentle breeze as much as
the next guy, but things were getting windy in a
Hurricane Hugo sorta way.

"What's happening?" Opera yelled. He would
have yelled, "Mhat's mappening," but the wind
was so strong that it had sucked the potato chips
right out of his mouth, giving new meaning to the
term *air pollution*.

"They've broken into the airplane!" Wall Street
shouted.

"Who?" Opera yelled.

"Wally's friends!"

"I don't see them!" I cried. "I don't—"

K-RASH
Thud Thud Thud

Suddenly, they dropped through the roof and landed in front of us. Talk about making an entrance. It was great to see the whole gang together again. I was particularly pleased to see Dad. Of course I wanted to leap up and run into his arms, but there was something about the way Tall Guy and Short Stuff shoved their weapons into my chest that made me a little shy about showing affection.

But not my dad. "Wally!" he cried. "Are you all right!?"

I nodded so hard you could hear my brains rattle.

"Son!" he shouted. "These men have something very important to tell you!"

"Zat's right!" Tall Guy cried. "Zings are not az zay appear! Vee muust talk to you."

I threw a nervous look up to Mr. Blond who was still standing in the front of the plane. They caught my glance and spun around to him.

"Zer hee iz!" Tall Guy shouted.

"He'z alive!" Short Stuff shouted back.

They pulled their weapons from my chest and spun around to Mr. Blond who began to yell, "The toothpaste, Wally! In your shaving kit, use the toothpaste!"

I reached down and started digging the toothpaste out of the kit.

The bad boys looked at me like I had a screw

loose. Who could blame them? There they were, holding their superautomatic, blow-you-to-kingdom-come guns, while I was grabbing my supertube of Whitey Bright Toothpaste . . . (regular flavored, not even mint).

"Squeeze it, Wally!" Mr. Blond shouted. "Pop the cap and squeeze it!"

I yanked off the lid and squeezed the tube. But instead of toothpaste, out shot a thick, gooey stream of what looked like . . . rope! Some sort of liquid rope! It squirted from the tube and instantly covered our two new guests. They shouted and tried to raise their weapons, but the rope was so sticky and strong that it bound their arms and hands, making it impossible for them to move.

"What are you doing?" Dad shouted. "You've got the wrong—"

But that was all I heard. Because as the bad boys struggled with the ropes, Mr. Blond broke into a loud, echoing laugh. "Excellent, Wallace. Simply excellent."

I nodded, giving the tube one last squirt (right in the middle, just in case either of them was a neat freak). Talk about being tied up in knots. Tall Guy and Short Stuff couldn't move a muscle.

I threw a triumphant look over to Dad, but instead of smiling, he was shaking his head.

"Well, gentlemen," Mr. Blond shouted, "I hate

to be a party pooper, but I have a few errands to attend to." He pulled out what looked like a miniature keypad from his pocket, hit a few keys, and his image started to flutter and waver.

"Oh, no," I groaned. "You did it to me again, didn't you?"

"Quite right, old bean." His image grew more and more transparent. "Now if you'll excuse me, it is definitely time to disappear."

And, just like that, he was gone.

Unfortunately, Tall Guy and Short Stuff weren't. They seemed more real than ever. And so was the truth Dad was about to share . . .

* * * * *

"What?" I cried. "No way!"

"I'm afraid it's true, Son." Dad looked me straight in the eyes. "Your friend, Mr. Blond, is the spy. He's the one our government is trying to catch. These gentlemen here," he motioned to the two men who were busy climbing and struggling out of the rope, "they're on our side. They're the good guys."

I couldn't believe it. You could have bowled me over with a Ping-Pong ball; with a piece of lint on a Ping-Pong ball; with a piece of dust on a piece of lint on a Ping-Pong ball—well, you get the picture.

"But . . . how?" I asked. "Are you sure?"

Dad nodded. "I checked with the FBI, CIA, NSA, and, of course, the PTA."

"But . . . but, I mean they're the ones who talk funny—not Mr. Blond."

"Zat iz becauze vee hav been hired by your government. Vee are zpecial double agentz."

"But . . . but, he seemed so sincere, so real."

"Az real az hiz holographic image?" Short Stuff asked.

I was beginning to get the picture.

"Zat's vhy vee hav been chasing you. To try and explain it to you."

I turned to Short Stuff. "You said you would 'blow me to kingdom come'!"

Short Stuff shrugged. "Juz a figure of zpeech."

"He'z been vatching too many late night cable moviez," Tall Guy explained. "Zorry if it frightened you."

"So what's really going on?" Wall Street asked.

"Yeah," I said. "Does that mean there isn't really a Giggle Gun?"

"And if there's no Giggle Gun," Opera frowned, "does that mean we won't get any more free junk food?"

"Actually," Dad explained, "before his death, Blond's partner stole the Giggle Gun and hid it in an African cave."

Tall Guy nodded. "Zat much iz true."

Dad continued. "But instead of risking his life to track it down, Blond figured he'd send you out to take the chance."

"But I'm just a kid."

"Ezactly," Short Stuff nodded. "Hee figured no von vould ezpect a kid."

I took a long breath and slowly let it out. "So he's been using me all of this time?"

"I'm afraid so," Dad said. "Ever since you ran into him at the Destructo Lasers—"

"Hey, that wasn't my fault!"

Dad simply looked at me. "Like it wasn't your fault that you tied these guys up a minute ago?"

"But . . . but . . ." There I was doing my famous motorboat imitation again.

Dad shook his head. "Wallace."

Uh-oh, now I was in for it. Whenever I became "Wallace" it was time to buckle in for another lecture.

"There's nothing wrong with making mistakes," he said. "People do it a dozen times a day. You tied up these fellows because you thought it was the right thing to do."

I nodded.

"It was a mistake, as simple as that. And it was a mistake when you ran into Blond at Destructo Lasers."

I started to argue, but he held up his hand. "That's okay, accidents happen all the time."

"But if I keep making them," I protested, "then you'll keep treating me like some immature kid."

Dad shook his head. "That's not true. Grownups make mistakes all the time. People only think you're immature when you don't admit to making them, when you don't take responsibility for them."

I looked at him and slowly started to nod. I think I was beginning to get it. "So," I finally sighed, "what do we do now?"

"Do you ztill vant to help?" Tall Guy asked.

"Well, yeah," I said. "I mean, it's the responsible thing to do, isn't it?" I glanced over to Dad to make sure he approved, but instead of smiling over how fast I was learning he was frowning.

"How dangerous would it be?" he asked.

"Not dangerouz at all. You vill be wiz hem zee entire time, and vee vill be monitoring your every move."

"And you're sure it's safe?" Dad insisted.

"Zer iz alvayz zome rizk," Tall Guy said. "But conzidering zee ztakez, it iz a rizk vee all need hem to take."

Everyone waited. After another moment, Dad slowly started to nod. "If you're sure it's necessary."

"Yez, I am afraid it iz." With that, Tall Guy turned to my friends and asked, "Vhat about you two? Do you ztill vant to cume?"

"You bet," Wall Street said.

"Do we get more chips?" Opera asked.

I threw him a look. He gave me a shrug.

"Vell zen, if you vant to help, if you vant to continue zis mizzion," Short Stuff said, "zen it'z important you appear *not* to believe our ztory. You muust pretend to ztill believe Mr. Blond."

"Zat's right," Tall Guy agreed. "Zen you can ztay in contact wiz hem. You can ztill pretend to help hem look vor zee Giggle Gun."

"Wow," Wall Street exclaimed. "That would make Wally kinda like a double agent?"

I swallowed hard. I hadn't been all that successful at being a single agent.

"Zat iz correct," Tall Guy said. Then turning his eyes intently upon me he continued, "If it'z vhat Vally vants."

I glanced around the plane. Now every eye was on me. I took another deep breath and slowly let it out. "Sure," I kinda half squeaked. "If you think you can still use me."

"All right!" Wall Street and Opera gave each other a high five (though I'm sure it had more to do with all the stuff they were getting than with my heroics).

I glanced over to Dad, whose reaction was slightly different. I couldn't believe it. There was actually moisture filling his eyes. Amazing. For the first time in the history of the human race, Dad was actually looking at me with pride.

I gave him a smile, and he reached out and tousled my hair. I knew he wanted to say something, but I knew he didn't trust his voice. I tell you there was more emotion flying around than in one of those "sense and sensitivity" movies Mom's always trying to get us to watch.

"So," I said, doing my best to swallow back the lump in my throat. "What uh, what exactly do I do?"

"Firzt vee muust stoop ovv at headquarterz. It'z deep in zee mountainz ov Zwitzerand."

"Switzerland!" Wall Street cried. "That's a major world banking center!"

"Switzerland!" Dad exclaimed. "I can buy your mother some great postcards!"

"Switzerland!" Opera hooted. "That's the home of Swiss chocolate!"

Yes sir, it seemed everybody was thrilled about the decision. Well, everybody but me . . . because, somewhere in the back of my mind, I suspected the fun and games weren't exactly over. And whenever the back of my mind suspects these things, I know the rest of my body will soon feel them in a major McDoogle mishap kind of way!

Chapter 7

Don't Forget to Floss!

Headquarters was at a secret airfield somewhere in the Swiss Alps. Once we landed they whisked us straight inside, which means we didn't get to see much scenery, but we sure got to see a lot of cool, superspy stuff.

After entering the lobby there were the usual superspy sliding doors; the long, superspy hallways; and of course your typical superspy body searches (which would have been a bit more typical if I wasn't so ticklish). I tried to warn them, but they weren't exactly in a wanting-to-be-warned mood. . . .

"Not *ho-ho-ho,* there *he-he-he.* Please I can't *har-har-har* breathe. My side is *tee-hee-hee* killing me. Oh no, *ho-ho-ho,* I'm getting sick. I think I have *har-har-har* to throw *ho-ho-ho . . .*"

(If you don't mind, I'll spare you this sound effect.)

After losing my cookies (or whatever in-flight snack they'd served on the plane) my body-searching pals let me go in an "Ooo grosss, get him out of here!" kinda way.

Next up was the superspy weapons room. Now this place was cooler than cool. It looked like it came right out of a James Bond movie (but without all the sex and violence). At the far end there were a bunch of targets. At our end there was a long, modern-looking table, with all sorts of computers and electronic gizmos.

Short Stuff had to leave and get something ready, so Tall Guy led us over to the table. As we took a seat he punched in a six-digit combination, and a small Plexiglas cube silently rose up out of the table. Inside were two rolls of extra fluffy, delicately scented . . . toilet paper.

That's right, *toilet paper.*

"You may vind yourzelf hafing to uze zis zome-time," Tall Guy said as he pulled one out and handed it to me.

"What is this, a joke?" I said.

He motioned to the toilet paper. "You hav had experienze wiz zis bevore?" he asked.

Wall Street and Opera snickered.

"Yeah," I said, feeling my ears growing hot, "I've had a little practice with it."

"Good," he nodded. "Juz make zure it'z ztrapped virmly to your body bevore lighting it."

"Strapped to my body?! Lighting it?!"

"Zertainly."

Seeing the surprised look on my face, he took the roll back from me and set it on the table. Next, he carefully pointed it toward a target about twenty feet away. Finally, he pulled out a match and lit the back end of the tube.

K-WOOOOSHHhhhh . . .

The thing shot from the table faster than a kid who's told he doesn't have to finish his broccoli.

"Wow," Opera cried. "Jet-powered toilet paper!"

"Impressive," Dad observed.

"This will give a whole new meaning to T. P.-ing somebody's house," Wall Street agreed.

Tall Guy pulled the other roll out of the Plexiglas cube. "Put zis in your shaving kit and be fery carevul how you uze it," he said as he handed it to me.

I nodded and gingerly placed it inside my kit.

Next, he entered another combination and another cube rose from the desk. Inside this one was a container of dental floss. He carefully removed it.

"What's this do?" I asked, reaching for it.

"Not zo fazt!" he cried, quickly pulling it away.

"Why? What is it?"

Without a word, he opened the top and pulled out about a foot of the floss. Then, taking aim at a nearby computer terminal, he flicked his wrist and snapped the end of the floss against the monitor.

K-BLAMB!

Everyone jumped in surprise. Well, everyone but me. I was too busy crying out in terror to remember to jump. When the smoke finally cleared, the fancy monitor was nothing but a smoldering pile of ash. We all stared at it in amazement as Tall Guy carefully closed the floss container and handed it to me. "Zis iz a fery powervul veapon," he said.

I swallowed hard. "And a good way to remove ugly plaque buildup, too, I bet."

Before he could respond, the doors hissed open and in walked Short Stuff. "Zis iz our latezt and mozt zpectacular invention of all," he said as he proudly approached.

I looked at it and blinked.

So did everybody else.

To be honest, it didn't look like anybody's most "zpectacular" anything. In fact, it looked exactly like—

"A taco?" Wall Street asked.

"This is your best invention?" Dad scowled.

"Does it come with extra cheese?" Opera asked.

"It only lookz like a taco," Short Stuff said as he carefully set it on the floor in front of us. He then reached into his pocket and pulled out three packets of hot sauce. He handed two of them to me and opened the third. "But vhen you add zis extra hot zauce . . ."

We crowded around as he opened the packet and carefully squirted a single drop onto the taco. To our amazement, it started to hum.

We stepped back a little.

He squirted on another drop. Now it began to vibrate.

We stepped back—a lot.

He finally gave the pack a big squeeze and squirted out the rest of the sauce. Suddenly, both sides of the taco shell folded down. Next, those same sides began to grow, telescoping out, becoming larger and larger, until each one looked like a giant four-foot wing.

But that was only the beginning . . .

Next, the center tomato slice began to expand, growing larger and larger, until it formed a round platform between the wings—a platform so big that a person could actually stand on it!

Meanwhile, the lettuce and cheese were doing their things as they grew into a set of handlebars

(complete with a little bike bell) and a dashboard
with all sorts of controls (but, unfortunately, no
CD player). In less than a minute the entire
taco had transformed into some sort of humming
vehicle with wings. And then—to our astonishment—the whole thing began to rise until it was
floating a good foot above the ground.

"What is it?" I cried over the hum.

"A hofercraft," Short Stuff shouted proudly. "It
iz our latezt invention. Vhat do you zink?"

"I zink it's pretty cool," I shouted.

"Pleaze," he motioned to me. "Ztep onto zee platform and try it out."

I threw a nervous look to Dad and my friends.
After all, they knew I was the master of disas-
ter. But they nodded for me to give it a shot. So I
carefully lifted my foot and stepped up onto the
floating hovercraft. It dipped slightly but easily
held my weight. I lifted my other foot, and in a
moment, I was standing directly in the center of
the floating platform. I grabbed the handlebars
and looked down at the controls. "What do all these
do?" I asked.

"Zat lever, zer, is vor your gearshift," Short Stuff
explained.

I nodded.

He pointed to other controls. "Here iz your aczler-
ator. Oh, and ov courz, your eight-track player."

(These guys may know about cool spy stuff, but they were a little behind in the car stereo department.)

"Let'z zee, I am forgetting zomezhing," he said frowning. "Vhat iz it . . ."

"Is it this switch here?" I asked, reaching for a red switch with a cover that read, "WARNING— DO NOT TOUCH!"

"No." He shook his head, without looking. "It'z zomezhing elze."

"Are you sure?" I asked flipping up the cover. "'Cause this looks pretty important."

"No," he scowled. "It'z zomezhing different."

"Well, what does it do when I flip it on?"

For the first time he glanced up and saw what I was doing. He opened his mouth, he started to shout, he started to scream—but he was too late. I had just flipped the switch.

K-VROOOOOM!
"AUGHhhh . . ."

The hovercraft shot off. Come to think of it, so did I (which would explain the AUGHhhh).

I hung on to the handlebars for dear life and tried to steer the thing as I zoomed back and forth around the room. I tell you,

K-SMASH! K-SMASH! K-SMASH!

other than a few destroyed desk lamps and computers

"LOOK OUT! HE'S COMING BACK!"

and my pals having to hit the deck every time I passed over their heads, I think I was starting to get the hang of it.

Still, there was one important thing missing. I looked over my shoulder and shouted back to Tall Guy, "WHERE ARE THE BRAKES ON THIS THING!?"

Short Stuff leaped to his feet. "Zat's vhat I forgot to tell you!"

"WHAT?" I cried.

"Zee brakez, zee brakez. Zay are over on your—"

But that was all I heard before

K-RASH!
splinter splinter splinter

I failed to make one very important turn, which meant I broke through one very important, superspy, sliding door.

Next, I shot down the very important, superspy hallway and past my superspy body searcher buddies . . .

"See ya," I gave a little wave as I finally sped out of the superspy front doors.

It was a beautiful day to take a little ride. The majestic mountains glistened with snow. The lovely, pastoral cows grazed pastorally on the pastoral, er, pastures. And the military cargo plane directly in front of me had its engines running and its cargo doors open.

Military cargo plane!?

I'm afraid so. I tried to pull up or swerve to the side, but I was too late. I roared through the door, into the plane, and . . .

K-POOF!

hit the wall. But it didn't hurt. In fact the crash was as soft and painless as the time I hit that extra-padded wall in Mr. Blond's old place. And for good reason . . .

"Good afternoon, Agent 00⅓th."

I immediately recognized the voice. With more than a little fear, I dug myself out of the wall and turned to see James Blond sitting at his desk.

"Take a seat and buckle in, Wallace. We're off to Africa."

Chapter 8

Africa!

Once again I was airborne, and once again I was hit by major *I-don't-want-to-be-doing-this-somebody-get-me-out-of-here-I-want-my-Mommy* kind of fear. It wasn't just my fear of heights, but my fear of flying around with a pretty bad, bad guy who claimed to be pretty good.

Of course Mr. Blond congratulated me on my cool getaway from Tall Guy and Short Stuff, and of course, I pretended like it was on purpose. (Sometimes being a double agent means not being as honest as you'd like to be.) Anyway, as far as I could tell, he didn't suspect that I knew the real truth, which was fine by me.

"Well," he said, as he headed toward the back of the cabin, "the flight will take a little while, so make yourself comfortable."

I swallowed hard.

"Is there anything wrong?" he asked.

"I hate heights, remember?"

"Of course," he smiled. "That's why I brought another replica of Ol' Betsy—to help take your mind off the flight."

I glanced beside my seat, and sure enough, there was another laptop computer, just like the others. "How many of these did you get?" I asked.

He grinned. "K-Mart was having a sale. Now, if you don't mind, I have some work to do. When we land, things will become a little busy."

"I just have one question," I said.

"You want to know if I'm real or another holographic image?" he asked.

Actually I was going to ask what the in-flight movie was, but since his question sounded a little more intelligent, I went with it instead. I nodded, and he immediately reached over to shake my hand.

With a little reluctance, I reached out and took his hand.

"It's nice to finally meet you face to face, 00½th." He grinned as we shook hands.

I also managed to crank up a little smile. The guy was definitely flesh and blood. This was good and bad—good because he would have to share whatever McDoogle mishaps were on their way, bad because flesh and blood spies usually have a way of hurting flesh and blood people.

So, with that extra little worry to be worrying in the back of my worrier, I braced myself as the plane took off.

Mr. Blond went to work at the rear of the cabin. And with nothing else to do except tie myself into knots (which isn't much fun unless you want to become a human macramé), I opened up Ol' Betsy IV and snapped her on to see what would happen to Gigabyte Guy . . .

As we rejoin our hero, he is fighting a computer character with teeth as big as Jim Carrey's. (Well, not that big, but almost.) The creature snaps and bites at him as Gigabyte Guy tries to explain how unhealthy in-between meal snacks can be—especially if they happen to be him.

And then, as luck would have it (along with some very clever writing from the author), our hero remembers the Control, Alt, Delete keys on his computer. It's a dangerous move, but the only one he has.

After a deep breath, he strikes the three keys. The computer begins shutting down all of its programs—including all alien monster games and all computer superheroes.

"All COMPUTER SUPERHEROES?!"

Great Gigabytes! If our hero doesn't get out of there fast, he'll be history. Within a nanosecond, he slips into the modem and e-mails himself directly to the computer of his archrival, Excuso Man.

Instantly, he zaps through the phone lines (except for the part where he has to wait half an hour for his Internet server). Once he arrives, he power surges his way through the computer all the way to the bad guy's monitor and takes a look. Mother of Megabytes! It's worse than he fears. In the lab he can see the diabolically devious, sinisterly slimy, and just the type to spit chewing gum out on the sidewalk where everyone walks...Excuso Man, who at that very moment is powering up his Excuse-a-tron.

In desperation, our hero leans back and rushes at the screen.

K-LUNK!

In a fit of major ignorance, he hits the glass just like he did back in chapter 5.

After making a note to upgrade his memory chip, he begins banging his fists on the inside of the screen. "Excuso Man! Excuso Man!"

The terrible tyrant turns and tosses a troublesome taunt. (Translation: He kinda yells.) "You're just in time, Giga Goon. All I have to do is fire this Excuse-a-tron Beam one last time and the entire planet will be polluted by its power. Soon, no one will be responsible again! Everybody will have an excuse for everything!"

Our hero searches his hard drive for some kind of solution. Suddenly his circuits recall the weakness of every bad guy who ever lived...pride. That's the thing that always gets 'em.

Turning up the volume on the computer's speakers, our hero shouts, "Those are pretty brave words, Excuso Man! Especially considering you're afraid to let anybody try to stop you."

"*Afraid?*" Excuso Man sneers. "I invited you, didn't I?"

"Only because you knew I couldn't get out of this computer to reach you. A real villain would have the courage to go one-on-one with his story's superhero."

Excuso Man laughs. "You actually think you could take me?"

"With one D drive tied behind my back."

"Talk is cheap, binary brain."

"That's right," our hero answers. "But do you see those virtual reality goggles and bodysuit over there? The ones conveniently placed nearby by our brilliant and incredibly clever author?"

"Yeah."

"If you put those on, you could enter my world, and we'd prove who was superior."

"I already know," Excuso Man scoffs.

"So prove it," Giga Guy challenges, "unless that Excuse-a-tron is also making you come up with too many excuses." He waits as the arch-antagonist starts to weaken. Finally, he goes in for the kill. "So, what are you?" he demands, "a man or a mouse? Come on now, squeak up!"

That's all it takes. Excuso Man's pride
is pricked, his arrogance is assaulted,
his machismo maligned. (Looks like it's
time to pull out the ol' dictionary,
doesn't it?) In a flash, the deranged
dude (there's another one) races to the
suit, slips on the goggles and gloves,
and prepares to meet our hero in cyber-
space. He crosses to the computer, hits
the Enter key, and suddenly...

Beep beep beep beep . . .

I glanced up from Ol' Betsy IV and looked
around, trying to figure out where the sound was
coming from. Mr. Blond heard it, too. In fact he
was already on the intercom shouting something to the pilot. When he was done, he turned
and slipped into the seat across from me.

"What's with the sound?" I asked.

He reached over to my trusty shaving kit
and pulled out the toothbrush. To my surprise,
the bristles were flashing and the handle was
beeping.

"It's the tracking device," he said. "The Giggle
Gun is right below us. Better buckle in, Wallace.
The pilot's going to have to drop in fast, so things
could get a little . . .

K-BAMB! K-RASH! K-SLAM!

. . . bumpy."

"What's happening?" I cried.

"There's no landing strip in the area! We're having to make our . . .

K-SLAM! K-RASH! K-BAMB!

. . . own."

"Isn't that dangerous?" I shouted.

"Nah . . . Just as long as we don't smash into any . . ."

K-SMASH!

Suddenly a giant tree ripped off our left wing and

K-RRREEEEKKKkkk

tore off the entire left side of the plane.

It was kinda interesting watching the African countryside pass by. And I might have enjoyed the tour, if I hadn't been screaming my head off. Then, of course, there was all my praying. Forget about emptying the trash and taking care of the cat box—now I was promising God I'd clean the entire house every week for the rest of my life!

And then, just like that, we came to a

K-THUDD!

stop.

"Well now," Mr. Blond cleared his throat and reached down to unfasten his seat belt, "that wasn't so bad, was it?"

I could only look at him. If this was his definition of "not so bad," I'd hate to be around when he thought we had some real trouble.

"Uh, Wallace?"

"Yeah . . ." I croaked.

"I think we have some real trouble."

I swallowed hard.

"Do you see that family of giraffes over there?"

I turned and looked out the ripped-off side of our plane. Just a few yards away stood a terrified baby giraffe. Beside him was one very startled mamma type. And beside her was one very angry dad.

"If I'm not mistaken," Mr. Blond continued, "I believe that bull giraffe there is about ready to attack us."

"What . . . what do we do?" I stuttered.

"Well first, I'd very carefully unbuckle my safety belt."

I did.

"Good. Next, I'd grab my shaving kit and slowly rise to my feet."

I did that, too. "Now what?" I asked.

"Well now, I think, it might be a very good idea to . . . *RUN FOR YOUR LIFE!!*"

With that bit of handy advice, Mr. Blond dashed down the aisle and leaped out of the plane. I did my best to follow—which wasn't a bad idea since papa giraffe had already begun to charge!

Once outside, leaves and branches slapped my face as I ran for all I was worth (which wouldn't be much if I became giraffe shoe goo). Meanwhile, the toothbrush in my shaving kit was going crazy.

BEEP BEEP BEEP BEEP BEEP BEEP

"Why's it doing that?!" I cried.

"We're right next to the cave!" Mr. Blond shouted.

"Are you sure it's a cave? I don't see anything!"

"Me either, but the tracking device can't be—"

"AUGHhhhhhh . . ."

Suddenly he disappeared from sight.

"AUGHhhhhhh . . ."

Without warning, I joined him.

After several seconds of tumbling and rolling out of control (not, of course, without the daily minimum requirement of bruises and broken bones), we finally came to a stop when we both hit

K-LUNK-"OW!"
K-LUNK-"OW!"

one extra hard, industrial strength rock.

Everything was very quiet and very dark. The reason was simple. I was very unconscious. When I came to, I could hear Mr. Blond moving around beside me.

"Are you okay?" he asked.

"Yeah," I groaned. "Just the usual broken body parts." I opened my eyes and saw it was even darker than when I was unconscious. "Where are we?" I asked.

"The best I can figure, we're at the bottom of the cave—with the Giggle Gun."

"How can you tell?" I rubbed my eyes, trying to peer through the darkness.

He lit a match and light flooded the cave. "Because, my dear Wallace," he broke into an ominous laugh, "I'm now holding it in my hand."

I squinted as my eyes adjusted to the brightness. Sure enough, in his hand was a cool-looking gun with all sorts of flashing gadgets and electric doohickeys.

He laughed again. It was a weird laugh—the type that gives you goose bumps.

"Is everything all right?" I asked.

"All right?" he sneered. "Everything is perfect. With this gun, I'll control the entire free world." He repeated his laugh and suddenly my goose bumps got goose bumps.

But he wasn't quite done.

"And you, my dear Wallace, Agent 00½th—or should I say *DOUBLE* agent?" He pointed the gun toward me and prepared to fire. "You shall be my first victim."

Chapter 9

Going Up?

So there I was in a dark cave, in darkest Africa, with the meanest bad guy I'd ever met. It's not that I minded darkness. I didn't even mind helping Mr. Blond out with his target practice—I just wasn't crazy about being the target.

And then, suddenly, I heard voices high above us.

"All right, Blond, zee game iz up!"

"Drop zee gun or vee blow you to kingdom cume!"

Yes sir, it was my old buddies from Switzerland. My heart skipped a beat. I had been rescued! I was safe! I was secure!

I was wrong . . .

With one swift move, Mr. Blond pulled me in closer and shoved the Giggle Gun into my ribs. "Try it," he shouted, "and I'll send this kid into eternal laughter!"

My heart pounded (more than making up for

that beat it skipped a couple paragraphs earlier). Don't get me wrong, I like a good yuck as much as the next guy, but suddenly the phrase "dying of laughter" had a brand new meaning.

Lucky for me, Tall Guy and Short Stuff seemed to agree. They reholstered their guns and waited for Mr. Blond to make the next move. Unfortunately, he did. He began dragging me with him up the steep slope of the cave.

Of course my pals tried the usual, "You'll nefer geet avay wiz zis!" And the ever popular, "Juz put down zee gun so vee can talk." But Mr. Blond had seen the same TV shows and wasn't about to fall for their cliché-riddled dialogue.

We continued toward the mouth of the cave. The good news was it was a lot less painful going up than going down. The bad news was it was a lot scarier with a Giggle Gun permanently attached to my side.

We reached the top. For a moment, the daylight blinded us. That's when my buds tried to make their move. But Mr. Blond cocked the Giggle Gun and shouted out his own cliché-riddled dialogue: "Everyone stay back or the kid gets it!"

My wannabe rescuers obeyed and stepped back. I tried it, too, but by the way Blond grabbed me, I guess he didn't exactly mean . . . *everyone*.

Now that we were out of the cave, he began

looking for an escape. Of course there was our trashed cargo plane, but it had more rips and twists than a piece of modern sculpture. Then he spotted it—the plane Tall Guy and Short Stuff had come in . . . a two-seater jet fighter.

"Let's go!" Blond growled as he dragged me toward it.

I knew the time had come. It was my chance to finally be a man, to show the type of courage I was really made of. It was time to drop to my knees and beg for my life: "Please, please, please, don't make me go up in that! Please, I'm scared of heights, remember. Besides, it wasn't my fault. They made me. I'm not the one that wanted to be a double agent—"

"Stop it!" he barked. "No one forced you into this mission. No one forced you to become a double agent. Those were *your* decisions, so take responsibility for them!"

Suddenly, he was sounding exactly like Dad— well, except for the shouting (and the Giggle Gun stuck in my ribs). But he was right. I was doing it again. I was using excuses.

He dragged me to the fighter and pushed me up the ladder toward the open cockpit.

"Get in the back!" he ordered.

I obeyed. There were a couple of parachutes on my seat, and I figured it wouldn't hurt to put one

on. Of course I practically choked myself to death
until I figured out where all the straps went. But
Mr. Blond paid no attention. He was too busy
standing up in the front of the cockpit and letting
go of some more sinister laughter. Then, just to
make things a little more interesting, he turned
the gun off of me and spun around and fired it
at Tall Guy and Short Stuff.

But instead of a *K-Bang! K-Boom!* or even the
ever popular *K-Pow!*, all I heard was

zing . . . zing . . . zing . . . zing . . .

as a fine mist shot from the gun and covered my
two buddies.

Slowly, they turned to each other. At first it
looked like nothing had happened. Then a tiny
giggle escaped from Tall Guy. Then one from Short
Stuff. And then one from both of them. They fought
hard, trying to keep straight faces, and they
almost succeeded—until Tall Guy burst into a
major case of the guffaws, followed, of course, by
Short Stuff's giggles. Now there was no stopping
them. Now they were going at it like a couple of
hyenas.

Mr. Blond and I traded looks.

But they didn't notice. They were laughing so
hard, tears streamed down their faces. Every once

in a while, when it looked like one was getting control, the other would bust out even louder, and it would get even worse. Soon they were doubling over, dropping their guns, and gasping for breath.

But Mr. Blond had other things on his mind. He turned to me and barked, "Sit down!"

I did. But my mind continued to race. I knew it was time to get back to taking responsibility. But what could I do? All I had was my shaving kit and . . .

Suddenly Mr. Blond fired up the jet's engines. Their piercing whine grew louder and louder, and louder some more. He pressed a lever and the cockpit roof automatically slid shut over our heads. We started rolling forward. I threw one last look over to Tall Guy and Short Stuff. They were flapping around on the ground, howling hysterically, and having the time of their lives.

I wish I could say the same for my life—whatever little was left of it.

We continued to roll, picking up speed, faster and faster, until Blond pulled back the stick and we shot up into the air. The force was so great that it shoved me deep into my seat. I was scared in a major *Scream XVIII* sort of way. But I was also determined. Even though I was petrified of flying, I was determined to be responsible. I was determined to do something, hopefully the *right* thing. But, even if

I failed, that was okay. At least I'd give it a shot—
and at least I'd take responsibility for it.

* * * * *

We were several miles up by the time I finally
quit praying. I had just added to my list of carry-
ing out the garbage, emptying the cat box, and
cleaning the house, by also promising never to fight
with my brothers and sister again. (Wait a
minute—am I out of my mind?!)

Because I was afraid of heights, I knew the last
thing in the world I should do is look out the window. So, of course, that was the first thing I did.

"AUGHhhh . . ."

That's about all you could hear of my scream
over the jet engines. Still, I knew I had to start
taking responsibility. But how? Where to begin?
All I had was the extra parachute that Blond
hadn't put on and my shaving kit. I opened up the
kit and started rummaging through it.

Let's see, there was my remote-tracking toothbrush. No, that wouldn't help.

How about my rocket-powered toilet paper?
Nah, probably not a good idea to shoot around
inside a jet fighter cockpit.

I pulled out what was left of the toothpaste tube.
It was almost empty—not enough to do anything,
except maybe play a game or two of cat's cradle.

I was starting to get nervous. I had to think of
something. The only thing left was the exploding
dental floss. Not a bad idea—if you wanted to blow
up the plane. Not a good idea if you wanted to live
to tell about it.

Wait a minute . . .

A plan slowly started to form. Carefully I pulled
off a few inches of the floss. I didn't want to blow up
the plane, but if Mr. Blond thought somebody else
was trying to, then maybe he'd get frightened
enough to set us down somewhere.

I took the floss in my fingers and gave it a
tiny little flick.

K-BAMB!

Perfect. I did it again.

K-BAMB! K-BAMB!

It did the trick. "They're shooting at us!" Mr.
Blond shouted.

I smiled. He was playing right into my hand.

K-BAMB! K-BAMB! K-BAMB!

"Brace yourself!" he cried. "I'm taking evasive action!"

I wasn't sure what evasive meant—until he threw us into a hard steep dive and a sharp right turn.

"AUGHHHHHHhhhhhh . . ."

Now I understood:

*Evasive: ē-vā-sĭve, adj. A method
of scaring your passengers to death.*

Blond wasn't going to land the plane. He was going to dodge the imaginary enemy by diving, spinning, and turning.

Uh-oh . . .

"Where are they?" he cried, as he brought us out of a steep power dive, then veered hard to the left. "I can't see them! I can't see them!"

I wanted to answer, to say the truth, but it's hard to say anything when your stomach is doing a pinball imitation inside your body.

Then suddenly, amidst the diving and turning, I spotted the Giggle Gun. It had come loose from Blond's side and was flying back toward me. I lunged for it. The good news was I grabbed it. The bad news was I grabbed the wrong part . . . the trigger part . . . the part that I accidentally squeezed . . . the part that accidentally fired the Giggle mist all over Mr. Blond.

zing . . . zing . . . zing . . . zing . . .

"Uh-oh" x 2

"WALLACE!?" he began to chuckle. "WHAT HAVE YOU . . . *Ho-ho . . . ha-ha . . . he-he* . . . DONE?!"
I was about to answer when he suddenly got the idea that things would be even funnier if he started flying the plane like a madman. Without a word (but plenty more laughter) he began taking us into a series of tight little loop-the-loops.

"Uh-oh" x 3

"WHOA . . . ," I shouted.
"HAR-HAR-HAR!"
"WAAAHH . . . ," I cried.
"HO-HO-HO!"
"EEEEEE. . . ."
But my screaming made little difference. By now he was laughing so hard he was doubling over. Then he was gasping for breath. Then he was accidentally grabbing the eject lever on his seat.
The eject lever on his seat?!

Yes sir, one minute Mr. Blond was in front of me flying the fighter. The next minute

K-CRASH!

his ejection seat fired, and he was shooting up through the cockpit and sailing high into the air.

The good news was Mr. Blond no longer had control over me. The bad news was that I didn't either. I was several miles high in a jet fighter, traveling six hundred miles an hour, without the slightest clue how to fly it. Then there was the other matter. The one of Mr. Blond tumbling toward the earth without a parachute.

Yes sir, things were not good in a migraine-maker kind of way.

And there was no one to blame but me.

Oh sure, I could have blamed the Giggle Gun for misfiring or Mr. Blond for hitting the ejection lever or anybody else for a hundred other things. But the truth was, I was the one who had pulled the trigger. I was the one who had gotten the two of us into this mess.

And instead of making excuses, I would continue taking responsibility until I got us out of it.

Chapter 10

Wrapping Up

At first I thought I'd try . . .

Plan A: Land the Fighter Myself.

After all, I flew the space shuttle way back in *My Life As an Afterthought Astronaut*. And now that I was so much older, I figured landing a jet fighter would be a piece of cake. (Hey, I said older . . . not smarter.) But since there was nobody around to talk me through the process, I went to my old standby . . .

Plan B: Panic and Scream for My Life.

I opened my mouth and:

(silence)

I tried again:

Ditto in the nothing department. (I guess it can be a little hard screaming into a six hundred mile an hour wind.) Now it was time for . . .

Plan C:

The only problem was I didn't have a Plan C.

All I had was the extra parachute I was still hanging onto and my trusty shaving kit. I looked back into the kit. I'd tried everything in it— well, everything but the rocket-powered toilet paper. And what good was rocket-powered toilet—

Wait a minute! That was it! Of course, I knew it would be risky and more than a little danger-ous. But what other choice did I have? More impor-tantly, what other chance did Mr. Blond have?

I strapped my shaving kit to my waist and slung the spare parachute over a shoulder. Even with the wind roaring in my ears, I could hear my heart pounding. Let's face it, it's not every day you leap out of a jet fighter to save somebody's life (while hopefully not losing your own).

I reached down to the eject lever beside my own seat, said one final prayer (no deals this time, just the standard: "PLEASE, PLEASE, PLEASE, HELP ME! HELP ME! HELP ME!"), and pulled.

WOOSHhhh . . .

I flew out of that cockpit faster than a junk food addict out of a health food store.

Even though I had two parachutes, falling toward earth was the last thing in the world I wanted to do. Actually the second to the last thing. The last thing was to do what Mr. Blond was doing—falling toward earth with *no* parachute.

I began searching the sky, looking for him, but he was nowhere to be found. Even though he'd only left the cockpit a few seconds earlier, there was nothing but sun and clouds and . . . wait a minute, what was that little speck way down there? That little speck that seemed to have two arms, two legs, and a head tilted back as if it were laughing hysterically?

Of course, it was Mr. Blond. He was pretty far away, but I wasn't worried. After all, we were miles and miles up in the air—and I had a plan. All I had to do was strap the rocket-powered toilet paper to my body, light it up, and zip down to him. Then I'd offer him the parachute and save the day. No sweat.

Except I had nothing to tie the rocket onto me with!

Then I remembered the toothpaste tube. Of course, why didn't I think of it! (Actually, I guess I did.) Somehow I managed to pull the tube from my shaving kit and give it a good squeeze. There wasn't much rope left, just enough to wrap it once around my body and tie the toilet paper to my back, which I did.

So far so good.

Now all I had to do was light the end of the roll and . . .

Wait a minute—I had nothing to light it with!

Wait another minute! (Good thing we had a couple of minutes to spare.) I suddenly remembered the dental floss. If I could snap just enough floss behind me to make a spark . . .

I dug into the kit, found the floss, and pulled off a few inches. Now all I had to do was reach around, snap the dental floss against the roll on my back, and fire up the rocket. A simple task for someone with incredible agility and strength. An impossibility for someone like me.

Still, I had no other choice.

I tried once and failed. I tried again with the same results. Part of me wanted to give up. But the other part, the responsible part, knew I had to keep trying.

And so I did. Again and again. And when I got tired of that, again some more, until finally

K-SNAP!
K-SPARK!
VA-ROOOOM!

The *K-SNAP!* was the floss finally snapping, the *K-SPARK!* was the floss finally sparking, and the *VA-ROOOOM!* was me finally, well, you get the picture.

I took off like . . . like someone with rocket-powered toilet paper strapped to his back. I tell you, it was pretty exciting to see a plan of mine actually work, like watching history in the making.

Mr. Blond, on the other hand, looked anything but excited. As I raced toward him, I could see he was still laughing, but his eyes were also growing wild with fear. I couldn't imagine why. Didn't he know I was coming to save the day? Didn't he see me rushing toward him at a gazillion miles an hour with no way to stop? *With no way to stop?*

(Now I got it.)

"Wally *he-he-he!* You're coming in way too *har-har-har.* We're going to—"

K-BAMB!

I smashed into him like a runaway freight train. In fact, we hit so hard that my toothpaste rope broke and the toilet paper shot up and away. Now it was just Mr. Blond and me . . . which was okay, except for the part where he was clinging to me like masking tape, covered in chewing gum, and topped off with Super Glue.

"Mr. Blond!" I cried. "Move your arm. I can't see where we're going!"

"Don't worry," he giggled. "I can see perfectly."

"Where are we headed?" I cried.

"Down." He broke into another fit of laughter.

"I have an extra parachute!" I shouted. "Can you slip it on?"

"This is no time for jokes," he laughed.

"No, I'm serious. Take a look." I motioned to the spare chute under my arm. "If you can take it and slip it on, you'll be okay."

He glanced down to my arm, then giggled. "No way would you do that for me."

"Of course I would."

"Why?"

"Because I was responsible for your pulling the eject lever."

"But . . . I'm your enemy." His laughter was starting to fade. "You should want me dead."

I shook my head. "I'm also supposed to obey God."

"What's that supposed to mean?"

"It means I'm also responsible for loving my enemies."

Thinking I was making a joke, he broke into another burst of laughter. But when he saw the look on my face, he slowly came to a stop. "You're serious, aren't you?"

I nodded.

He looked down at the parachute one last time and then back up to me.

I motioned for him to take it.

He hesitated and then reached out to grab it . . . which was a pretty good idea, considering that the ground was a lot closer than it had been—and getting closer by the second!

He quickly strapped himself into the chute and then looked back to me. The effects of the Giggle Gun had nearly worn off. I could tell by the look in his eyes that he was really moved by what I'd done. He wanted to say something, but it was obvious he couldn't find the words.

I nodded to him, making it clear that I understood.

He nodded back. And then, without a word, he let go of me and pushed off.

I watched as he sailed away. After he was fifty or sixty feet from me, he pulled his rip cord, and

K-WOSH!

his chute shot out and opened, while I zipped past him like a sack of potatoes (or at least a sack of Wallys).

I decided to follow his example. I fumbled for my own rip cord, gave it a tug, and

K-WOSH!
"OAFF!"

my chute opened and tugged so hard that I thought the straps were going to rip off my arms. And then, suddenly, I was floating. No screaming wind in my ears, no falling toward the ground at a bazillion miles an hour. Nothing but blue sky and a gentle breeze. Talk about peaceful. And what a view. It was incredible. There was nothing between me and the earth except—

Nothing!

I glanced over to Mr. Blond who was steering away from me as fast as he could. And for good reason. When I looked back down, I spotted Tall Guy and Short Stuff directly below me. With all of our aerobatics it looked like we'd managed to dive and circle all the way back around to where we had started.

I could tell by their actions that they were also recovering from their giggle attack. I knew that they'd be hoping I'd have the Giggle Gun and that they'd be upset when they found out I didn't. But the last I saw of it, it was going down in flames with the plane, which was kinda unfortunate. Then again, maybe it wasn't. Maybe it was for the best. After all, if something caused this much trouble, maybe it was better that nobody had it.

I also knew Tall Guy and Short Stuff would be anything but thrilled about Mr. Blond getting away. In fact, they probably looked at the whole operation as being one, gigantic failure. Maybe they were right.

Then again, maybe they weren't. After all, I did come back with one thing. I finally understand the importance of responsibility. Granted, maybe it wasn't some fancy, secret weapon to save the world—then again, maybe it was. Because if everybody practiced it, if everybody took responsibility for what they did and for helping one another, the world would be a lot better off.

I glanced back to the ground. It looked like Tall Guy was on a cell phone. I hoped he was calling Dad and Opera and Wall Street to let them know I was okay. Maybe he was even making arrangements to get us all back together again. By the look of things, I had a few more minutes before I landed. And since there was nothing else to do (except worry about how many sprained legs I'd be collecting in that landing), I thought I'd try and finish my Gigabyte Guy story. I didn't have Ol' Betsy I, II, III, or IV, but I figured it wouldn't be that hard to think up an ending in my head.

So I gave it a shot . . .

When we last left our story, the extreme and excessively icky Excuso Man had just slipped on his virtual

reality gear and was about to duke
it out with our hero. The baddest of
bad boys reaches for the ENTER key,
hits it, and suddenly appears on the
computer screen directly behind
Gigabyte Guy.

"All right, Giga Geek!" he cries.
"Prepare to meet your match!"

Our hero spins around just in time to
see Excuso Man press his Laser Blaster
Wristband (sold in leading toy stores
everywhere) and

Zip Zip Zip

Gigabyte leaps out of the way just as

K-BLAM! K-BLAM! K-BLAM!

the beam hits the desktop publishing
program directly behind him.

Our hero staggers back to his feet,
but he barely has time to reboot before
Excuso Man leans back and hurls his
Turbocharged Electrolights (sold in
those same toy stores) at him.

Zap Zap Zap

K-CRACKLE! K-CRACKLE! K-CRACKLE!

Again, Gigabyte Guy leaps out of the way, as an old solitaire program bites the dust.

But Excuso Man isn't finished yet. Next, the crummy cyber creep pulls out his Electrocharged Light Saber and——

"Hold it! Wait a minute!" our hero cries.

Excuso Man lowers his saber. "Is there a problem?"

"Well, yeah." Gigabyte climbs back to his feet. "I mean, doesn't all this seem pretty violent?"

"What do you mean?"

"Laser Blaster Wristbands... Turbo-charged Electrolights."

"This is a superhero story. What do you expect?"

"I know, but kids will be reading this stuff, right?"

"Right."

"Well, doesn't it seem just a little bit, oh, I don't know...irresponsible to be putting so much violence in a story for kids? I mean, what if they get the wrong idea? What if they actually think that violence is the best way to solve problems?"

"But,...but we're super action fig- ures," Excuso Man argues. "Super action figures are *always* violent."

"Unless, of course, we wanted to start a new trend. Unless, of course, we wanted to start being...*responsible*."

"Hmm..." Excuso Man begins scratching his 256-bit colored hair on his 3-D ani- mated head.

Gigabyte Guy continues, "Wouldn't it be better if we were to work out our differences? You know, talk them over and see if we could reach a compromise?"

"Yeah, but if we did that, we'd have to admit we'd been wrong during all those other pages."

"True, but wouldn't it also be responsible to admit that we've been wrong and try to fix it?"

Excuso Man begins to nod. "Yes... you have a very good point." He glances out of the computer screen, thinking of all the future readers. "It's true, we should be setting a good example."

Gigabyte Guy nods. "Exactly."

"So what do we do?"

"I say we admit we were wrong and sit down over a nice bowl of crashed hard drives and discuss our differences. That way we can prove to our readers that violence isn't the answer. What do you think?"

Excuso Man hesitates. "Of course, I could think of a hundred excuses but..." Finally, he breaks into a grin and reaches out to shake our hero's hand. "I'm with you, Gigabyte Guy."

"That's incredibly keen," exclaims our hero. "And, might I add, just super-duperly swell."

After selecting a beautiful sunset from an old clip art program, the two stroll arm and arm toward it, knowing that together they will find a way to solve their differences. Together they will find a solution that is safe, fair, and (although pretty corny and not as dramatic as blasting someone to smithereens) they will find an ending that is (here it comes)...*responsible*.

"Mizter McDoogle! Mizter McDoogle!"
I glanced down. Tall Guy and Short Stuff were

frantically waving their arms. "You're cuming in too zteep. Pull back on zee control linez, pull back on zee linez."

Of course, I had no idea what they were talking about. I was lucky just to have my parachute open, let alone trying to control it. I gave one last thought to my superhero story. It was a little on the heavy-handed side, but responsibility is a pretty heavy topic. I thought back to what Dad had said about everyone making mistakes. And how the surest sign that I'm growing up is when I admit that I've made a mistake and try to fix it.

"MIZTER McDOOGLE, LOOK OUT! YOU ARE GOING TO LAND RIGHT ON TOP OV UZ! YOU'RE GOING TO LAND RIGHT ON—"

K-SMASH! K-SMASH!
"OAVV!" "OAVV!"

Needless to say, it was a perfect landing—right on top of their heads. I'll save you the painful details (as if you couldn't guess). Still, it was great to see my old pals again. And it was just like old times as we began sorting out various body parts and broken bones.

"Exzcuze me, Mizter McDoogle, pleaze take your elbow out ov mine ear."

"Oh, sorry."

As we pulled ourselves together, I realized another important truth—

"Say, is that my kneecap over there?"

I realized that even though I was growing up and becoming more responsible, it was nice to know that some things about me—

"You're zitting on mine head!"

"Oh, sorry."

"Now you are ztepping on mine ear lobz!"

"Sorry, sorry."

It was nice to know that some things about me would never change.